10·3·95

DRUGS AND GUN VIOLENCE

Drug use can increase violent tendencies in even the mildest-mannered person.

THE DRUG ABUSE PREVENTION LIBRARY

DRUGS AND GUN VIOLENCE

Maryann Miller

THE ROSEN PUBLISHING GROUP, INC.
NEW YORK

Published in 1995 by the Rosen Publishing Group, Inc.
29 East 21st Street, New York, NY 10010

First Edition

Library of Congress Cataloging-in-Publication Data

Miller, Maryann, 1943-
    Drugs and gun violence / Maryann Miller. — 1st ed.
      p.   cm. — (The drug abuse prevention library)
    Includes bibliographical references and index.
    Summary: Examines the relationship between drugs and gun violence in modern society.
   ISBN 0-8239-2060-7
    1. Drug abuse and crime—United States—Juvenile literature. 2. Alcoholism and crime—United States —Juvenile literature. 3. Violent crimes—United States—Juvenile literature. 4. Firearm ownership— United States—Juvenile literature. [1. Drug abuse and crime. 2. Violence. 3. Violent crimes.]
    I. Title. II. Series.
    HV5809.5.M55 1995
    364.2'4—dc20   95-5910
                                 CIP
                                 AC

Manufactured in the United States of America

Contents

Introduction

Kevin was the second son in a large middle-class family that included three brothers and a sister. He liked sports and music and hanging out with his friends. He didn't much care for school, but he did his best. If he didn't, his father would be all over him.

But when Kevin was 14, a friend introduced him to a marijuana joint. It was cool. It clouded his mind so that he didn't have to think. He didn't have to remember that his older brother was dead, killed in a freak car accident. And of all the miseries of his teenage years, that was the one thing Kevin wanted to forget forever.

After a while the marijuana didn't help so much, and Kevin started using LSD. Then he tried heroin, and finally crack cocaine. To

Drugs that most people consider mild, such as psilocybin ("magic" mushrooms), can lead to the use of stronger, more dangerous drugs.

support his habit, he turned to robbery and burglary, starting with his own home. When Kevin was 16, his parents kicked him out. They couldn't keep on buying new TVs to replace the ones he stole.

Out on the streets, Kevin met other addicts, who showed him how to survive. They planned and carried out burglaries together. They watched out for each other. And they bought guns.

At first the guns were only to protect themselves. They figured they needed them; a guy doesn't last long on the streets if he doesn't show how tough he is. Then they got

One joint can put you on a downhilll road.

the idea to use the guns in robberies. Instead of stealing stuff and pawning it, they could rob liquor stores and gas stations. They would get a lot more money for a lot less time and effort.

What Kevin didn't count on was getting sent to prison for murder. They weren't supposed to shoot anybody. The guns were only to scare the guy into giving them the money. But Randy was flying on crack. He thought it would be cool to see the guy blown apart just like on TV.

It wasn't cool. It was devastating. That moment in time ended one life and ruined countless others. Everyone associated with it suffered in some way. A wife lost her husband. A mother lost her son. A child lost a father. And Randy and Kevin lost their youth in a federal prison.

All because of drugs and guns. The greatest tragedy of drugs is that no one sets out to ruin his life. People convince themselves that the horrors they see on the news won't ever happen to them. They think, "What can it hurt? One little joint?"

Long-term drug use can cause several mental health problems, including outbursts of aggression.

CHAPTER 1

The Reality of Drugs

*T*he problem with one little joint is that it can lead to addiction. Many people develop a chemical addiction to a substance the first few times they try it. Then that isn't enough. Their body starts demanding more of the drug, and then other drugs. That's when things can start getting out of hand, as they did with Kevin.

In addition to physical dependency, some people form a psychological dependency. Like Kevin, they want to block something out of their mind. They think that zoning out with drugs is the answer.

Long-range drug use can cause a number of mental health problems. Some of these problems are distortion of perception/reality, mental confusion, irritabil-

12 | ity, outbursts of aggression, and paranoid thinking. Many people also have bouts of depression that can lead to suicide or attempted suicide.

Personality disorders also can develop. Paranoid psychosis is a disorder that causes feelings of persecution. People become suspicious of others without any reason. Another disorder is compulsive behavior, which causes nervousness and irritability. Compulsive people repeat actions and are unable to sit still. Such disorders can lead to bizarre and often violent behavior.

The Most Common Drugs

Stimulants

Commonly called "uppers," these drugs— marijuana, amphetamines, cocaine, and crack cocaine—act on the central nervous system to create a "high." They increase the heart rate, blood pressure, and body temperature. Frequent use can cause heart attacks and strokes.

Marijuana is sometimes listed as both a stimulant and a hallucinogen. Its physical effects are like a stimulant. It has also been known to cause hallucinations, especially when used with another drug.

Amphetamines are considered stimulants.

Cocaine and crack are more addictive than marijuana. Use of both drugs has risen dramatically in the United States in the past ten years.

Methamphetamine is a stimulant with effects similar to those of cocaine. On the street it is known as "speed," "crank," "crystal," or "crystal meth." People who use this drug often "binge," then experience a "crash." During the crash they can suffer depression, irritability, anxiety, and insomnia. In extreme cases, it can also cause a psychosis similar to paranoid schizophrenia.

14 | ## Barbiturates

Commonly called "downers," these are usually used as sleeping pills and muscle relaxants.

Barbiturates are highly addictive. The body's tolerance level builds quickly, so that users need more of the drug to achieve the same results. Barbiturates are also extremely dangerous when used with alcohol. Both substances reduce respiration and lower the blood pressure, which can lead to coma and death.

Tranquilizers

Tranquilizers are used to control anxiety. Two of the common ones are sold as Librium and Valium. They are legally dispensed by prescription but are also available on the streets illegally. These drugs slow your body's functions and make you feel mellow. If you get too mellow, your heart could stop.

Narcotics

Narcotics are used legally as painkillers. Morphine is one of the strongest painkillers. It can be addictive, and doctors are very careful in prescribing it. People have become addicted to morphine after using it to control pain in surgery or

Cocaine, crack, and heroin are just a few of the drugs sold illegally on the street.

severe injuries. Legal narcotics are often stolen from hospitals and sold on the streets illegally.

Heroin and opium are illegal narcotic drugs. They are used to get a "high" that lasts longer than the one from cocaine. The high can last up to six hours. It is followed by a "crash" that can last for days. Heroin, like crack, can be immediately addictive. The longer the addiction, the more of the drug is needed to satisfy the craving.

Hallucinogens

LSD, known as "acid," has been used widely since the 1960s. PCP, "angel

16 | dust," has been around as long but became more popular in the '70s and '80s. These drugs distort reality. They can make you see and hear things that aren't there and make you believe you can do impossible things. Marijuana joints can be "laced" with LSD or PCP without your knowing it. These drugs are especially dangerous because on a "bad trip" many young people die in accidents.

PCP can also produce paranoia, intense anger, and hostility. Some experts believe it causes more violent behavior than any other drug.

Alcohol

Some people don't consider alcohol a drug, but it is. However, public intoxication and driving under the influence (DUI) are illegal. So are possession and use of alcohol by minors. Alcohol is not immediately addictive, but it does have immediate effects. It upsets the normal working of your central nervous system. That's why people stagger and slur words when they are drunk.

Alcohol can make you very sick if you drink too much. For many young teens getting drunk for the first time, their fun ends when they get violently ill and pass

Alcohol affects everyone differently.

out. There is also a danger of alcohol poisoning. If you weigh about a hundred pounds and drink a whole bottle of wine, your body can't process all the alcohol. Because the alcohol is toxic, you could go into shock and die.

Many people don't realize the danger of alcohol and guns combined. "You put alcohol and firearms together and you account for 50 to 75 percent of all adolescent deaths," says Dr. Barbara Staggers. Dr. Staggers is in charge of the Teen Clinic of Children's Hospital in Oakland, California. She also has clinics at two high schools in Oakland, one in the inner

18 | city and one in an up-scale suburb. At both clinics she counsels or treats teens with problems of drugs, violence, gangs, and unprotected sex.

Inhalants

Inhalants include a wide variety of substances, including glue, gasoline, paint thinner, nitrous oxide, and ether. They are used primarily by young people who can't afford or don't have access to other drugs. Inhalants are also abused by children as young as eight or nine. By sniffing (inhaling through the nose) or huffing (inhaling through the mouth) an inhalant, a person gets a reaction similar to that of taking other drugs.

We would have to live on a remote desert island not to know some of the dangers of drug abuse. Many of us have even seen the danger firsthand. We had a friend or maybe even a family member who overdosed. We knew someone who committed suicide while high on some drug. Or we knew someone who was killed in a car accident after a night of drinking at a party.

Those dangers, however, are only the beginning.

CHAPTER 2

Gun Violence

In his early teens, Marco joined a gang. He thought it would be good to belong. At age 14 he started carrying a gun. It came in handy when he started working for a Jamaican "posse," or drug gang. His job was to make sure everyone paid and no one stole money or drugs from the bosses. The job made Marco feel very important. But then one day some money was missing. The bosses thought Marco had taken it, and he knew he was in big trouble. He thought he knew who had the money, so he took his gun and confronted the boy. Marco says he doesn't know why, but he shot and killed the boy. "I didn't have to kill him," Marco said. "If I'd just pulled the gun, I could have gotten the money."

20   Ten or twenty years ago, a story like that would have caused a national stir. People didn't just shoot other people for no reason. Today, however, Marco's story is commonplace. People are killing other people at alarming rates in the United States:

- In 1991, 38,317 people—more than 100 people a day—were killed by firearms. These deaths included homicides, suicides, and accidents.

- An average of 14 children and teenagers are killed with guns each day.
- A child or teenager commits suicide with a gun every six hours.
- Firearms kill more people between the ages of 15 and 24 than all natural causes combined.
- In 1990, 4,173 teens were killed by guns in America. This number includes homicides, suicides, and accidental shootings.
- From 1986 to 1991 the homicide rate among those 14 to 24 rose by 62 percent. Among those 14 to 17, the rate rose by 124 percent.
- Firearm murders committed by teens under age 18 increased from 444 in 1984 to 952 in 1989.

- A 1993 Justice Department report
  found that the most frequent victims
  of firearm violence are between the
  ages of 16 and 19. Their risk of
  being shot to death has more than
  doubled in the last decade.
- FBI crime figures for 1993 showed
  that the overall violent crime rate
  dropped by 1 percent, but the homicide rate rose by 3 percent.

Not all of these deaths and violence
are drug-related. Some are caused by
disputes over other issues. Some are even
accidental. But many of them are linked
to drug use or drug-related business,
and that number is growing. Alfred
Blumstein, a professor at Pittsburgh's
Carnegie Mellon University, blames the
drug wars. "Over the last seven years, we
have seen a major growth in the presence
of guns, largely stimulated by the number
of young people in the drug business who
have guns."

Making the Connection
A link between drugs and crime has
always existed. Drug users commit four
to six times as many crimes as nondrug
users. A 1990 FBI report showed that

22 | almost a third of the persons convicted of robbery and burglary did the crime to get money for drugs. The same report showed that the number of drug-related homicides grew from 19,257 in 1986 to 20,045 in 1990.

A similar report in 1989 showed that 36 percent of victims of violent crime said they believed their assailants were under the influence of drugs.

A 1987 study showed that 83 percent of youths in long-term state-operated juvenile facilities admitted some drug use; 63 percent of them said they used drugs regularly. The most common drugs reported were marijuana, cocaine, and amphetamines, and use started as young as age 10.

Twenty percent of these young offenders also said that they had used guns while committing a crime, and 45 percent said they were on drugs at the time.

A 1993 report showed that people who were involved in selling drugs had high levels of gun ownership and use. Sixty percent were very likely to carry a gun during drug deals. Sixty-three percent said they had fired a gun during those deals.

Another report showed that criminal

Many gang members feel they have to be armed.

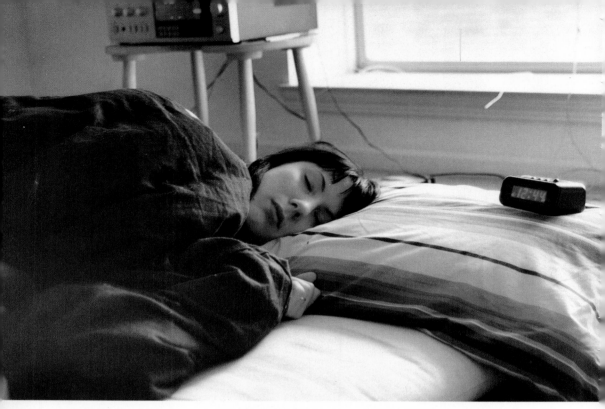

Drug use wastes your life away.

activity was high among frequent users of heroin or cocaine. It was two to three times higher than the rate for irregular users or nonusers of drugs.

That study also showed that as drug use increases, the number of crimes committed also increases. A person starts out smoking a little "weed" and lifting money from his mother's purse. In a year or so, he could be mainlining heroin, stealing cars, and robbing gas stations.

A 1986 study of crime in New York showed that 78 percent of men arrested for serious crimes were also cocaine users, an increase of 42 percent from

1984. According to the commander
of the New York Police Department
Narcotics Division, "There's no question
there's a close correlation between the
recent increase we've experienced in violent crime, and the increase this study has
shown in the use of drugs."

How Do Drugs Cause Violence?

Most research points to three causes of
violence associated with drugs:

1. **Pharmacological Violence.** That
thousand-dollar word simply means violence committed by a person using drugs
at the time of the act. A study in New
York showed that some drugs can cause
users to "become excitable and/or irra-
tional" and "act out in a violent manner."

Drugs can also give the user the
courage to commit an act of violence. By
altering reality, they can help a person
believe that what he or she is doing is not
wrong. That's what happened to Marco.
To him, what he was doing was like tele-
vision or a movie. It wasn't real, so it
couldn't be wrong.

Drugs are also used sometimes to give
a person the courage to do something
known to be wrong. This is common in
gang initiations. Many young members

26 | are terrified at having to participate in a drive-by shooting, but they won't let on to the other members. They try to mask their fear in drugs so they can do what they have to do to belong.

2. **Economic Compulsive Violence.** This is violence that occurs while an addict is trying to get money to buy drugs. The need for money has motivated criminals to rob and steal since the beginning of time. What is different today is the violence associated with those crimes. People are often assaulted or killed during a robbery, mugging, or burglary. It is avoiding the truth to say it has nothing to do with an increase in drug use and easy access to guns.

3. **Systematic Violence.** This is the violence associated with the buying and selling of drugs. It includes protecting a territory, which is commonly known as "turf war." Turf wars are often the reason for drive-by shootings. This kind of violence also includes robbery of dealers, elimination of informers, and assault to collect debts.

A study in Detroit showed, however, that not all drug violence occurs to get money. Gang members talked about

"Zero action." To them, a "Zero" is a person who doesn't care about anything. He has nothing to lose and is capable of extreme violence. One gang member said of Zeros, "They ain't afraid to die over any stupid thing. They like to rape babies, beat up people, and kill somebody for fun."

Members of a drug-dealing gang in Oakland talked about their violence toward rivals as "gunning and funning." And one Zero said, "I likes seeing little scared preppies when we beast on their [asses]. My crew is the beasting crew . . ."

A study in England shows that addicts turn to crime and violence for other reasons. In London there are clinics where addicts can get drugs legally. Yet many continue to commit crimes and buy drugs illegally.

Thus, people enjoy flirting with the dangers of the illegal drug world. This is particularly disturbing because it moves drug violence out of areas that can be understood and explained. Even though we don't approve of an addict mugging a senior citizen for her Social Security check, at least we can understand why it happens. With this new type of antisocial behavior, the "why" defies understanding.

CHAPTER 3

Big Business

"**D**rug trafficking is the single most serious organized crime problem in the world today."—President's Commission on Organized Crime, 1986.

Since the drug trade is illegal, it is hard to determine how much money is involved, but some experts estimate that tens of billions of dollars are made every year. Records show that one drug ring in New York made $151 million in a four-year period. That's a lot of money, and people will do anything to protect it. That's why the drug business is so dangerous.

Regular business has a number of legal ways to enforce contracts and punish people who violate agreements. People can be taken to court and forced to

Gangs involved in the drug business are especially dangerous.

honor contracts. That can't happen in the drug business, so the dealers protect their business in other ways—frequently with violence.

- If a dealer holds back money in a drug sale, the supplier often has him killed.
- If someone tries to move in on a dealer's territory, the dealer has him killed.
- If an outsider tries to interfere with gang/drug business, he is killed.

A dealer's first job is to get new customers hooked on whatever he is selling.

Running the Business

Since 1989 the production of heroin and marijuana has decreased steadily. Production of cocaine has increased, however. It is estimated that 250 tons of cocaine enter the United States each year, but many experts believe that figure is low.

The drug trade is primarily controlled by organized crime. When we think of organized crime, we think first of the Mafia, and it was indeed responsible for organized crime in America.

The Mafia came to power during Prohibition, when the manufacture and sale of alcoholic beverages was illegal. Criminals in the United States "organized" to take advantage of Prohibition. From 1919 until 1933, when the law was repealed, the Mafia grew rich and powerful by smuggling and selling alcohol.

In 1931, Salvatore Luciano, known as Lucky Luciano, organized the local "families" to form a "Commission." The Commission made decisions about business and settled disputes among the Mafia families. Loyalty to the family and obedience to the "bosses" was expected of every member.

When alcohol was no longer illegal, some Mafia families moved into other drugs, although most steered clear of the drug trade until recent years. Luciano directed the importation of heroin and set up a distribution system. He was a large part of the drug trade until his death in 1962.

The Mafia, portrayed in movies like the *Godfather* series and *Goodfellas*, still exists and controls some of the drug trade. Other organizations—the Jamaican Posse, Chinese Triads, the Vietnamese Born to Kill, and many others—have all made inroads into the business since the '70s. That has created the turf wars that contribute to much of the street and gang violence in our towns and cities. As one law-enforcement official

32 | puts it, "We have more people fighting over the same piece of pie."

The Players

The drug trade is international. The drugs themselves are grown in countries in the Middle East, South America, Central America, Mexico, Asia, and Cuba. Then they are smuggled by different routes into the United States.

There are key people in the drug business. The *drug lord* handles the growing, harvesting, and processing of some drugs. The drug lords have great power in their countries. They have "armies" to protect the crops from local authorities. Assault weapons manufactured in the United States arm the drug cartels in Colombia. Some weapons are taken from supplies intended for legal deals, and others are smuggled into the country.

To protect their business, the drug lords send *hit teams* to other countries. One such team was discovered in Canada in 1989. Police in Edmundston, New Brunswick, stopped a car and a van on a quiet residential street. The vehicles contained an Uzi submachine gun, two assault rifles, and 3,000 rounds of ammunition. By the next day, five men, all carrying Venezuelan passports, had been arrested. The men were believed to be Colombians on a mission to free or silence two other Colombians charged with importing cocaine into Canada. The drug lords intended to eliminate any possibility that the business could be traced to them.

Not every gang in the drug business operates the same way. They are not all so highly structured. But most of them follow a pattern pretty closely.

The sale of drugs is controlled by a *distributor* or a *supplier*, sometimes called the "main man." He receives the smuggled goods from the *importer* and sells them to the dealers. (Importers receive the drugs into the country. They also take them into countries, as the Colombians were doing in Canada.)

Dealers use teens and young gang members as *lookouts, spotters*, and *couriers*. Members are allowed to sell small quantities of drugs. They also act as *enforcers* or *shotguns*, protecting the dealer and guarding the operation from theft. This is a very dangerous role, and most enforcers end up injured or dead in a few years.

Every step of the way—from drug lord to the guy on the street—guns are in-

Drug sales are the source of much of the world's violence.

volved. They are often stolen and used to pay for drugs, and they are easy to get on the streets. According to a chief homicide detective in Oakland, "We wouldn't have a murder problem if it wasn't for drugs."

The violence associated with drugs is not limited to the United States. In Panama, the homicide rate has soared since 1990. From about 100 a year in the '80s, it climbed to 296 in 1991. Colombia had a homicide rate of 29,000 in 1991. In Venezuela, the number of weekend slayings tripled in four years. The primary factor in all these killings is the drug trade.

Drug use is also high among Panamanian teens. Crack houses are a common sight, and crack violence follows. "Teenagers get so hooked on drugs they don't want to work. And they lose their minds," says Hector Escudero. "They'll kill for 50 cents."

Escudero knows what he is talking about. He works for a funeral parlor in Panama City where business is tragically booming. In the '80s he used to pick up one or two bodies a day, usually people who had died of illness or old age. Now he picks up at least five a day and more on weekends. Most of the bodies he picks up now were victims of drug violence.

So Why Do They Do It?

If being involved with drugs and the drug business is so dangerous, why do people continue to do it?

Research done in London indicates that "the attraction of the drug scene is as much social as chemical." Drugs can provide status and a sense of identity in addition to an imagined way out of life's difficulties. For some young people, belonging to a drug-dealing gang is a kind of security that they don't have anywhere else. They believe they matter to

36 the other gang members, and that makes them feel important.

There is also a sort of romance associated with the drug business, especially for very young teens. They see the drug trade as a way to make a great deal of money and gain power and prestige. One report said, "Some are in it for money, and some are in it because they want to be *noticed*, or they want people to have respect for them."

A study of Miami crack dealers drew an interesting conclusion. It saw the way dealers act as "reminiscent of descriptions applied some years ago to the heroin-user subculture—the joys of hustling and 'taking care of business,' the thrills of a 'cops and robbers' street life."

Unfortunately, there is a big difference between the "hustlers" of the '50s and '60s and those of the '90s. Violence has increased, and so has the appeal of violence. In the old days it was the use of drugs that was the status symbol. You were "cool," you belonged, if you did drugs.

Now, doing drugs is not enough. Now it is the willingness to participate in violent acts that determines status. You have to be tougher than the next guy and not afraid to use a gun.

CHAPTER 4

An Invitation to Trouble

*I*n 1994, a Midwestern girl of 17 ended her long association with drugs and crime by fatally shooting another teenage girl. She is charged with first-degree murder and use of a firearm to commit a felony. Awaiting trial as an adult, this girl is headed for prison instead of college.

Everyone who picks up that first joint is not necessarily going to prison, but the potential is there. Drugs can make you do things that would be unthinkable under other circumstances. They cloud reality so that sometimes you don't even know what you are doing.

The real tragedy in this story, and many like it, is the innocent victim. People who are not doing drugs or

38 involved in the drug business are killed every day. Neighborhoods, schools, and even our own homes are no longer safe from drug violence. Anyone, anywhere can be a victim of someone else's addiction and use of a gun.

Homicide

In a study of drugs and homicide, Paul J. Goldstein reported that the homicide rate in the United States increased slowly after World War I. It jumped dramatically during the period of Prohibition and leveled off after Prohibition was repealed. The homicide rate took another dramatic rise in the early 1980s and continues to rise:

> In 1985, 21 percent of the homicides reported in Washington, D.C., were drug-related. That grew to 34 percent in 1986, 51 percent in 1987, and 80 percent in 1988.

The fact that drugs and homicide are related simply cannot be disputed. Too many statistics prove it.

Random Acts of Violence

Drug-related homicides occur in a variety of situations.

Drug addicts must often resort to violence to get money for their next fix.

These are often the most shocking and hardest to understand. They may be shooting sprees or massacres. In either case, the killer usually has no connection with the people killed. They are just targets.

Some homicides are connected to other crimes, such as burglary or robbery. In many cases, there is no reason to kill while committing the crime. But if the criminal is under the influence of drugs, the chances are greater that he will kill than not kill.

A tragic example happened in New York in 1988. A 17-year-old crack addict

40 robbed and shot five people in a six-hour period one day. The next day he robbed three stores and shot five more people. After two more days of violence, the police finally caught the teenager. At that time, it was the worst juvenile crime spree in the city's history.

Drive-By Shootings

People are no longer safe even in their homes. In nearly every city in America, the sound of gunfire is common. Innocent people are caught in the crossfire between drug dealers and anyone trying to move into their territory.

A five-year-old mistakenly shot by a drug dealer . . . a two-year-old hit by a bullet that came ripping through her apartment wall . . . a twelve-year-old who just went out to get the mail . . . a pregnant woman sitting at her kitchen table . . .

The number of people killed or injured in drive-by shootings grows year by year. Whole neighborhoods are frozen in fear as drugs, gangs, and violence take over the streets.

Accidents

Drugs also cause many accidental deaths

and injuries, especially among young
people. A few friends get together and
have a couple of beers or smoke a little
crack. Then they start fooling around
with a gun, talking big and acting macho.
Pretty soon someone is dead, and someone else is saying, "I didn't mean to do it.
God, I didn't mean to do it!"

Many hunting "accidents" can be
traced to drug abuse. For some, the
annual hunting trip is just an opportunity
to hang out with friends and drink as
much as possible. They go out into the
fields and shoot anything that moves.
Sometimes it's the friend they were just
drinking with.

There is a parallel between the rise of
drug use in America and the violence rate.
Meanwhile, the availability of guns has
also increased:

- From 1960 to 1980, the population
  of the United States increased by 26
  percent; the homicide rate due to
  guns increased 160 percent.
- An estimated 200 million firearms
  are owned by civilians in the United
  States. Handguns outsell rifles and
  shotguns.
- In 1991 on an average day in the

42

United States, 135,000 children carried a gun to school.
- Guns have replaced knives and other weapons as the weapon of choice among teens.

Guns can be bought on the street for as little as $30, and anyone who wants one knows how to get it. Dealers will take a gun in payment for dope, then sell the gun for a profit. In some cases guns have been rented. In Los Angeles alone, two men sold more than 1,000 handguns in an eight-month period.

CHAPTER 5

Drugs, Gangs, and Guns

*D*rugs = money.
Gangs = family.
Guns = power.
Drugs + gangs + guns = disaster.

That's an equation you won't see in math class, but it's certainly worth thinking about.

Gang-related killings are swiftly becoming the number one concern of law-enforcement officials across the country. And it's not just a big-city problem. Smaller towns and rural areas are sharing in the concern.

Mayors from small towns took their concerns to a U.S. Senate committee meeting in 1991. One mayor had this to

Drugs are big business.

say, "Drug dealers from cities are opening rural 'branch operations,' complete with landing strips . . . and arsenals of assault weapons for security."

The spread of big-city gangs into other areas has been a problem for at least ten years. The reason is drug money. The two largest gangs in the Los Angeles area have sent members into almost every major city in the United States to set up the business. One law-enforcement official describes this as "franchising. It's just like the fast-food industry."

At first, the franchising went on 44 primarily in cities like Miami, Dallas, and

Phoenix. Then the gangs started moving into small towns in the Midwest and the South. They introduced drugs and the drug business to the young people there. Soon guns and violence followed.

Lieutenant Robert Dacus, who heads the Gang Unit in the Omaha Police Department, has seen the problem grow since 1988. "When I came on board, we had about 300 gang members," he says. "Now we have about 1,100."

Dacus says it is difficult to give an exact number of gang members who are involved with drugs. But the presence of drugs in the area has grown in relation to the growth in gang members.

One of the main reasons the big-city gangs take drugs to new markets is money. "An ounce of cocaine that sells for $300 in L.A. will go for $1,500 here," Lt. Dacus says. "That's an incredible profit. And even when we arrest the out-of-town dealers, there's someone here who can't resist the lure of big bucks."

Criminal gangs, or structured gangs, are more likely to be involved in drugs and gun violence than unstructured gangs. Criminal gangs share the following characteristics:

46

- Formal membership, with a required initiation and rules for members.
- A recognized leader or certain members whom others follow.
- Common clothing, group colors, symbols, or tattoos, and a special language.
- A group name.
- Members from the same neighborhood, street, or school.
- Turf or territory where the group is known and where its activities usually take place.

A survey of state prison inmates in 1991 had some interesting information about gang membership, drugs, and violent crime. The study compared inmates having previous gang membership to those who did not belong to gangs. Of the gang members, 92 percent said they fought regularly with other groups. For the nongang members the rate was only 26 percent.

Of the gang members, 69 percent said they manufactured, imported, or sold drugs as a group. Among the nongang members, 37 percent committed drug offenses together.

The growing number of gangs and the

aging of gang members contribute to in- **47**
creased violence. Older gang members
are more likely to be involved in
homicides.

Known gang membership in the United
States almost doubled between 1989 and
1991, jumping from 120,636 to 202,981.
Eighty-seven percent of gang members are
Hispanic or African-American, and they
dominate the criminal gangs. Gangs of
white, Cambodian, Chinese, Korean,
Laotian, and Vietnamese youths are on the
rise, particularly in Chicago, New York,
and Los Angeles. There has also been a
significant increase in female gang membership.

Using a gun is often part of gang
initiation. One boy who joined a gang
when he was 13 said guns were everywhere. He started taking part in drive-by
shootings as soon as he joined the gang.
"My friends would call me their little
gangster," he says. "With the gun I felt
like I couldn't be stopped."

This boy's story was told by Gordon
Witkin in *U.S. News & World Report* in
1991. "Much of the fuel for the growth in
youth violence flows from gangs and
drugs. Not nearly as many teens would
have guns if they hadn't raised the money

48 by dealing drugs, nor would the streets be so violent these days in the absence of drug trade," Witkin concluded.

Unstructured gangs are not usually heavily involved in the drug business. The gangs are smaller, and the members are usually "wannabes," young people who want to be in a gang. Often they are used by the structured/criminal gangs as spotters, lookouts, and couriers, which puts them at greater risk of arrest if the police show up.

The older gang members are really using these young people to avoid the harsh adult penalties for dealing in drugs. The danger for the young people, however, is just as great. They can get killed by someone who is trying to take the drugs away from them. They can get killed by rival gang members trying to take over a new territory.

Because of those dangers, more young people are getting and using guns. According to a Los Angeles police officer, the rise in homicides in that city resulted from "territorial disputes among gang members who all want the privilege of selling cocaine."

CHAPTER 6

Gun Violence Goes To School

"I was hallucinating a little bit, you know. Thinking there was people behind me, following me. I was doing a little bit of leaving trails. Playing with my trails. Like with your hand moving through the air, it leaves a trail. Then I thought I heard voices, you know, calling me, and . . . I just got this crazy idea: Shoot the principal. He came after me, I thought he was a monster or something. Can't remember that well. I just shot, you know. He went down to the ground."

That incident was related by a teenage boy in *Dope and Trouble* by Elliott Currie. When the boy took the gun to school, he was high on LSD. Luckily for him and

50 | the principal, the gun was only a pellet gun, so the boy did not end up in prison for murder. He was sent to a correctional facility, which is where Currie met and interviewed him.

Guns and drugs come to school primarily in two ways. Students who are high bring a gun to right some real or imagined wrong. Or they may be just acting out some deep frustration like the boy quoted above. He had a long history of problems at school and at home, coupled with long-term drug abuse. It all just came together in one horrible explosion the day he shot the principal.

Guns are also part of the drug-dealing scene at many schools. In a 1993 study of drugs and guns, students who were selling drugs reported more gun activity than those who were not involved with drug use or drug selling.

Ronald D. Stephens wrote in *USA Today Magazine* (January 1994), "The issue of weapons in schools cannot be addressed adequately without considering the impact of gangs and drugs; they are inseparable."

In that same issue, another article reported on the problem of weapons and violence in schools:

Gun-related violence is affecting students in all grades, including students in elementary and middle school.

- One in five elementary school and one in four middle school principals cite growth in gun-related incidents.
- One in four elementary school principals cites an increase in gang activity in the schools.
- Drugs and alcohol are often considered as major contributors to incidents of school violence.
- More than one in four elementary school principals note a rise in alcohol-related incidents.

A report in *TEEN* (July 1993) listed the main causes of gun violence in schools:

Drugs/gangs—18%
Long-standing disagreements—15%
Playing with or cleaning guns—13%
Romantic disagreements—12%
Fights over possessions—10%
Depression—9%

The article included stories from students who had experienced or witnessed gun violence in or near school.

I was walking home from school one day. My high school is right near an elementary school. My friend and I were right near the elementary school when we saw these two kids—one was a girl, and one was a boy. They looked like they were still in elementary school. We were walking and the boy all of a sudden pointed a gun at us . . . This boy was just pointing it at us, just trying to show us that he had a gun . . . and that he wasn't afraid to use it. But my friend and I just kept walking . . . as if nothing had happened. The girl was saying, "Stop it! Stop it! It might go off."

It didn't hit me until I got home. Then I thought, "I could have died." I just started crying and crying.

The other stories related similar concerns. Students were afraid. They were upset over the senseless death of friends. They were worried that it might not end soon.

The Problem Keeps Growing

As drug use and violence on the streets increase, they are becoming a greater problem in schools. What does this all mean for the average student? At the very least, it disrupts the learning environment. Students are becoming more concerned with their safety than with their classes. Teachers are becoming more concerned with maintaining safety and control than with what they are teaching.

But the major problem of violence in school is still personal safety. Students are reminded of the threat every time they walk through a metal detector to enter school. They are again reminded when they have a "gunfire" drill, learning to hit the floor at the sound of gunshots.

These measures do not make the students feel secure. They only increase their fear, and that fear is causing more and more young people to get guns for protection. They don't realize that they are adding to the problem. They're just looking for a way to feel safe again.

Conclusion

*S*ome of the information in this book is pretty depressing. It makes it sound like a hopeless situation. Do we just try to find a safe corner somewhere and cover our head?

That's a tempting thought. But no problem gets solved by hiding from it. In most cases, you have control over your own life and destiny. You can choose not to pick up that first marijuana cigarette or take that first hit of crack. You don't have to join a gang or buy a gun to show how tough you are.

CBS aired a special program (April 26, 1994) that dramatically illustrated those choices. Titled "Kids Killing Kids," the program showed four conflicts that ended in violence. Then each conflict was replayed with a resolution that did not involve a gun.

The incidents dealt with the most common situations in which young people use guns. A youth tries to keep a gang away from his brother. A boy carries a gun to school to impress a girl. A depressed teenager has easy access to a gun and commits suicide. A teen takes a gun to school because he has been hassled and frightened.

It's hard to say how effective such programs are. But like any other effort made to stem the tide of violence, if it saves one person, it is worth the effort.

"Kids Killing Kids" is available on videocassette, and most Blockbuster Video stores offer the tape at no charge. Perhaps it's worth checking out and watching with a few friends. It could help you take control of part of your life.

Even in those areas where you have less control, there are things you can do. Work to make your school and your neighborhood drug-free. People everywhere are taking their neighborhoods back. They work with the police and other agencies to keep the drug dealers out.

Don't be afraid to inform authorities

56 about kids who bring drugs and danger into your school, but do so *carefully*. They won't hesitate to kill you if you get in their way. Are they worth your protection?

You can also promote mediation programs in your school to solve conflicts before they get violent. The Satellite Academy, in the South Bronx area of New York City, has been using a very successful mediation program. Called "Resolving Conflict Creatively," the program teaches students how to solve problems without violence.

For information about mediation programs, write to:

School Mediation Associates
72 Chester Road
Belmont, MA 02178

A helpful support group is SAVE (Students Against Violence Everywhere). Similar to SADD (Students Against Drunk Driving), it can be established in any school. For information, write to:

SAVE
West Charlotte Senior High School
2219 Senior Drive
Charlotte, NC 28216

Glossary
Explaining New Words

addiction Constant need to use a drug.

amphetamines Drugs that speed up the central nervous system; called *uppers*.

barbiturates Drugs that slow down or depress the central nervous system; called *downers*.

cocaine Powerful stimulant made from the leaves of coca plants.

crack Crystalline preparation of cocaine, usually smoked.

hallucinogens Drugs that make you see and hear things that aren't there.

heroin Opiate produced by chemical modification of morphine.

LSD Drug that produces hallucinations.

methamphetamine Stimulant with effects similar to cocaine.

morphine Opiate used as a sedative and painkiller.

narcotic Painkiller such as those derived from poppies: opium, morphine, or heroin.

paranoid schizophrenia Mental disorder characterized by delusions and sometimes hallucinations.

58 **pharmacological** Pertaining to drugs or the science of drugs.

physical dependence Adaptation of the body to the presence of a drug.

psychological dependence Condition in which a drug user craves a drug to maintain a sense of well-being and feels discomfort without it.

psychosis Serious mental disorder characterized by deterioration of intellectual and social functioning and by partial or complete withdrawal from reality.

tolerance Decrease of physical reaction to the effects of a drug.

Help List

The following are organizations available for help relating to drugs and/or violence.

Alcoholics Anonymous
15 East 26th Street
New York, NY 10010
1-800-662-HELP

Narcotics Anonymous
P.O. Box 9999
Van Nuys, CA 91409
818-780-3951

National Council on Alcoholism and Drug Dependence (NCADD)
12 West 21st Street
New York, NY 10010
212-206-6770

National Black Alcoholism Council, Inc.
1629 K Street NW
Washington, DC 20006
202-296-2696

60 | ## American Council for Drug Education
204 Monroe Street
Rockville, MD 20850
301-294-0600

National Clearinghouse for Alcohol and Drug Information
P.O. Box 2345
Rockville, MD 20852

National Families in Action
2296 Henderson Mill Road
Atlanta, GA 30345
404-934-6364

Resource Center on Substance Abuse Prevention and Disabilities
1331 F Street NW
Washington, DC 20004
202-783-2900

TEEN-LINE
1-800-999-9999
Sponsored by Covenant House, this is a hotline to call with concerns about gun violence. It focuses on suicide, but teens can call with other concerns.

For Further Reading

Adint, Victor. *Drugs and Crime*. New York: Rosen Publishing Group, 1994.

Currie, Elliott. *Dope and Trouble*. New York: Pantheon Books, 1991.

———. *Reckoning: Drugs, the Cities, and the American Future*. New York: Hill and Wang, a division of Farrar, Straus and Giroux, 1993.

Goode, Stephen. *Violence in America*. New York: Alfred A. Knopf, 1980.

Hoobler, Thomas and Dorothy. *Drugs and Crime*. New York: Chelsea House Publishers, 1988.

Landau, Elaine. *Teenage Violence*. New York: Harcourt Brace Jovanovich, 1966.

Louria, Donald B. *The Drug Scene*. New York: McGraw-Hill, 1968.

Miller, Maryann. *Coping with Weapons and Violence in Your School and on Your Streets*. New York: Rosen Publishing Group, 1993.

Salak, John. *Drugs in Society*. New York: Twenty-First Century Books, 1993.

Seixas, Judith S. Drugs: *What They Are*

62

and What They Do. New York: William
Morrow & Co., 1991.

Webb, Margot. *Coping with Street Gangs,*
rev.ed. New York: Rosen Publishing
Group, 1995.

Index

About the Author

Maryann Miller has been published in numerous magazines and Dallas newspapers. She has served as editor, columnist, reviewer, and feature writer.
Married for over thirty years, Ms. Miller is the mother of five children. She and her husband live in Omaha, Nebraska.

Photo Credits

Cover photo: by Michael Brandt; all other photos by Yung-Hee Chia.

Design by Blackbirch Graphics